The
boy
in the
biscuit
tin

The boy in the biscuit tin

Heather Dyer

Illustrated by
Peter Bailey

Chicken House

2 Palmer Street, Frome, Somerset BA11 1DS

Text © Heather Dyer 2007
Illustrations© Peter Bailey 2007

First published in Great Britain in 2007
The Chicken House
2 Palmer Street
Frome, Somerset BA11 1DS
United Kingdom
www.doublecluck.com

Cover design by Ian Butterworth
Cover illustration by Peter Bailey
Designed and typeset by Ian Butterworth
Printed in the UK by CPI Bookmarque, Croydon CR0 4TD

3 5 7 9 10 8 6 4 2

British Library Cataloguing in Publication data available.

ISBN 978 1 905294 28 2

The author would like to express her gratitude to Hawthornden Castle for the fellowship she was awarded there in 2004.

CHAPTER 1

Magic For Beginners

"Francis?" said Ibby. "Can I come in?"

There was no reply, so Ibby knocked twice and opened the door. But to her surprise the room was empty. There was only a black top hat rolling gently on the carpet as though its owner had departed in a hurry.

Ibby checked in the wardrobe and under the bed, then she went to the window and looked out. But there was nobody there. Francis appeared to have vanished.

Ibby went downstairs again and found Aunt Carole and her parents in the front room, having tea.

"Here she is!" said Aunt Carole, smiling. "Did you find Francis?"

"No," said Ibby. "He's disappeared."

"He's probably just hiding. Here – have a biscuit."

"Thanks," said Ibby, and she took a chocolate-covered wafer and a glass of orange juice, and went and sat beside her mother on the couch.

"You're quite a young lady now, aren't you?" remarked Aunt Carole. "Your hair's getting ever so long."

"Too long," said Ibby's mother, tucking Ibby's hair behind her ear. Ibby had a pale, rather serious face and long fair hair, which she liked to wear loose like her friend Shareen. (Her mother made her wear it back for school. She said it looked untidy otherwise.)

"Are you still a big reader?" asked Aunt Carole.

"Oh, yes," said Ibby's father. "Ibby always has a book on the go, don't you, Ibby?"

"I wish the boys liked reading," said Aunt Carole. And then the conversation moved on to

Alex and his website, and then to Francis and his karate classes.

Meanwhile, Ibby nibbled her chocolate-covered wafer and looked around. Aunt Carole's shelves were full of tatty books, and there was a vase of peacock feathers, a sheep's skull, and other things that Aunt Carole and the boys had collected on their walks.

Normally, Ibby liked staying at her aunt's house. But this time it was different. This time she was staying on her own.

"You won't be on your own," her father had told her. "Alex and Francis will be there too."

But Ibby didn't find this very reassuring. The last time she had seen her cousins was when they had all gone to stay at a bed and breakfast in the Lake District. Alex hadn't wanted to come on holiday at all, and had traipsed after them everywhere with his head down, playing an electronic game that beeped every time he scored a point. Francis, on the other hand, had barely been able to contain his excitement and had kept them all awake at night by slamming doors and running up and down the stairs. On the second night he had got his finger stuck in the shower drain, and everyone had come out onto the landing in their dressing gowns to watch while the ambulance men carried him off with the shower tray still attached to the end of his finger.

Ibby's mother said Aunt Carole let the boys get away with murder, but Ibby's father thought Aunt Carole did her best. After all, he said, it couldn't be easy bringing up two boys alone.

Especially boys like Alex and Francis, Ibby thought. But she'd said nothing.

Just then, Ibby's thoughts were interrupted by a crash directly overhead, and the sound of furniture being dragged across the floor.

"Goodness!" said Ibby's mother. "What's going on up there?"

But before Aunt Carole could answer, someone yelled "MUM?" and feet came pounding down the stairs. A moment later Alex appeared in the doorway. "Have we got any tins?" he said.

Alex must be practically a teenager now, thought Ibby. Unlike Francis (who was one of those people who can't help looking untidy) Alex was one of those people who can't seem to help looking smart. His dark hair was longer on top and parted in the middle, and when he ran

his hand through it, it always fell neatly back in place. (Francis had dark hair too, but his always stuck straight up in front as though a cow had licked it off his forehead with a big wet tongue.)

"What sort of tin do you want?" asked Aunt Carole.

"Something with a lid."

"Will a biscuit tin do? There's one in the pantry on the top shelf. But put it back when …"

But Alex had already gone.

"Well," said Ibby's mother, getting up. "I suppose we'd better be off. We've got to register by four o'clock."

Ibby's heart sank. So this was it. Her parents were leaving her here for four whole days while they attended a technical writing conference in Cardiff.

"Be good," said Ibby's mother.

Ibby said nothing. She was always good.

"We'll be back before you know it!" said her father. Then they went outside and got into their car, and Ibby's father started up the engine and her mother wound the window down and blew a kiss.

Ibby and Aunt Carole waved from the front

step as the car went down the drive. Then it turned the corner and was gone.

CHAPTER 2

The Boy In The Biscuit Tin

"THE STEP-BY-STEP INSTRUCTIONS ARE EASY TO FOLLOW."

Ibby went back upstairs. Francis's bedroom door was firmly closed and there was a lot of banging and crashing coming from within. "Francis?" said Ibby. She knocked twice and went in.

"Shut the door!" barked Alex. "Don't let it get away!"

"Let what get away?" said Ibby, startled.

"I don't know." Alex was on his knees, peering under the bed. "Some sort of mouse, I think. With stripes."

"Stripes?"

Then out from under the bed darted a small figure – no larger than one of the people from Ibby's dolls' house. It ran across the carpet directly in front of Ibby's feet, and disappeared under the armchair – but not before Ibby had recognized Francis's scruffy brown head and stripy sweater. She stepped backwards with a cry of astonishment. *Francis*?

"Push!" yelled Alex, throwing his weight against the chair.

"Don't!" shrieked Ibby. "You'll squash him!"

But to her relief, where the chair had stood there was only a dusty square of carpet on which lay a green plastic soldier and a broken pen.

"Where'd it go?" said Alex, looking round.

"There!" said Ibby, pointing – and before Francis could disappear under a landslide of board games and jigsaw boxes, she pounced. When she stood up she was trembling, with her hands cupped close to her chest.

"Let's see!" said Alex.

Slowly, Ibby opened her hands – and there was Francis, curled up in a ball.

There was a shocked pause. Then Alex said, "What is it?"

"It's Francis," said Ibby.

"Francis? What's happened to him?"

"He's shrunk."

"I can see that. But how?"

At the sound of their voices, Francis uncurled and started trying to scramble out of Ibby's hands. "Pass the tin!" said Ibby. "Quick!" So Alex brought the biscuit tin and, carefully, Ibby released Francis into it. Immediately he went rushing round and round inside the tin, trying to scramble up the reflective silver walls in a hopeless sort of way.

"What's he doing?" said Ibby anxiously. "Why's he running round and round like that?"

"Small animals do everything quickly," said Alex. "They've got a higher metabolic rate. That's why they're always hungry. If shrews don't eat their own weight in worms every hour they can starve to death."

"They starve to death in an hour?" said Ibby, shocked.

"Or quicker, even."

"Let's put the lid on. Perhaps he'll go to sleep."

"We can't do that! He'll suffocate!"

Alex ran downstairs and came back with a

chocolate biscuit, a saucer of water, and a few
lengths of toilet paper. He arranged everything
in the tin, whereupon Francis promptly
knocked over the water, ignored the biscuit, and
began bundling up lengths of paper.

"He's making a nest," said Ibby. "Look!"

But Alex was looking at something else.

His gaze had fallen on a long black box, lying
on the floor. On the front of the box it said:
Magic for Beginners, and there was a picture of
a white rabbit jumping out of a black top hat.

Beneath the picture it said:

ASTONISH YOUR FRIENDS AND CHARM YOUR GIRLFRIEND
WITH THESE INCREDIBLE MAGIC TRICKS! THIS BEAUTIFULLY
PRESENTED SET INCLUDES A TOP HAT, CLOAK AND ALL THE
PROPS YOU NEED TO PERFORM YOUR VERY OWN MAGIC SHOW.

"I knew it," said Alex.

"Knew what?"

"He's been doing magic!"

"Magic sets don't do real magic," objected Ibby. "They're all about sleight of hand and false bottoms, and things …" She trailed off uncertainly. She had just remembered the black top hat rolling gently on Francis's bedroom carpet.

"It's the only explanation," said Alex. He broke off a tiny piece of biscuit and held it over the tin, making kissing noises. Presently the mound of paper trembled, and a hand appeared. It took the biscuit and withdrew.

"Right," said Ibby suddenly. "I'm going to tell Aunt Carole."

"No! We can't do that!"

"Why not?" said Ibby, hesitating.

"Well – think of the shock it would give her! And she won't be able to *do* anything, will she?"

"She might," said Ibby, but she looked unsure.

"She won't," said Alex firmly. "She'll rush him straight to hospital. They'll do all sorts of tests on him and then when nothing works they'll take him to a laboratory and put him in a cage

21

with lots of white rats."

"They wouldn't!"

"Yes, they would. That's what always happens in cases like this. It'll be on the news and in all the papers and he'll be known for ever afterwards as 'The Boy in the Biscuit Tin'." Alex put his arm round Ibby's shoulders and led her back to the bed, where she sat down reluctantly.

"So what do you think we should do?" she asked.

"Make him big again, of course."

"How?"

"With the magic set."

"Oh! Do you think we can?"

"Of course we can," said Alex reassuringly. "Where are the instructions?"

22

CHAPTER 3

The Magic For Beginners Helpline

"CALLS CHARGED AT PREMIUM RATE."

Ibby found the Magic for Beginners instruction booklet and turned to the table of contents. There were seven tricks listed:

1. Amazing Miniaturization
2. Levitation
3. The Multicoloured Handkerchief
4. The Disappearing Coin
5. Cards
6. The Life Cycle
7. The Vanishing Act

"Amazing Miniaturization!" cried Ibby, and she flipped to page three and found six numbered steps, each accompanied by a tiny illustration of a magician "tipping his hat" or "taking a bow" or waving his wand in a certain way. But the final step said simply: Tap object with wand three times and hey presto! The object has been miniaturized. That was all. It didn't say whether the effects of the trick were permanent or not – nor how to reverse it.

"It doesn't tell you anything," said Ibby.

Alex didn't answer. He was examining the black top hat. It was clever the way it collapsed into a disc, then popped up again when you gave it a twist.

Ibby frowned and turned to the back of the booklet instead. In small print on the very last page there was a disclaimer. Here is what it said: All magic tricks are undertaken at the magician's own risk. Please call the Magic for Beginners Helpline for further information.

"There's a number to call," said Ibby. "Quick! Alex, get your phone."

"It's only for emergencies," said Alex. He was trying on the top hat in front of the mirror. It looked best, he decided, worn slightly forwards, at an angle.

"This *is* an emergency!"

Alex sighed, but he strode out of the room and reappeared a moment later with his phone. "Don't use all the credit," he said.

Ibby dialled the number. After several rings, there was a click, and a woman's voice said: "Welcome to Magic for Beginners. Please choose one of the following options: To purchase Magic for Beginners, press one. For careers with Magic for Beginners, press two …" The recorded message continued, until eventually the voice concluded by saying: "… and for assistance, please hold."

Ibby waited. Some xylophone music came on. Every now and again the woman's voice returned, saying: "Please hold, and your call will be answered as soon as possible."

"A lot of people must need help," said Ibby gloomily.

Alex glanced at his watch. At last the voice returned. "Hello!" it said. "Welcome to Magic for—" Then the line went dead.

"I got cut off!"

Alex snatched his phone and peered at the display. "You've used up all my credit!"

"Never mind your credit!" cried Ibby. "What about Francis? You don't care about him at all, do you?"

"Yes, I do!"

"No, you don't!"

"Don't be silly," said Alex. "Of course I care. All I'm saying is – hey! Wait!"

But Ibby had already snatched up the biscuit tin and gone running downstairs, shouting, "Aunt Carole! Aunt Carole!"

Before she got halfway down the stairs, however, Ibby lost her footing. The tin flew out of her hands, and the next thing Ibby knew she was falling head first down the stairs.

The first thing she saw when she got to her feet was Francis. He was sitting large as life on the fourth stair, brushing bits of tissue paper out of his hair.

"Francis!" she cried. "Are you all right?"

"I think so," said Francis, rubbing his head.

"See?" said Alex, from the top of the stairs. "I knew he'd be OK."

But just then Aunt Carole rushed out of the kitchen. "What happened?" she cried. "What was that big crash?" She looked at Francis, who had a long red welt on his forehead where the edge of the biscuit tin had caught him – then at Alex, who looked suspiciously like a person who had just pushed someone down the stairs.

"Well?" she said. "Would someone like to tell me what's going on?"

For a moment, nobody spoke. And then (as often happens when the real crisis has passed) Ibby burst into tears and told Aunt Carole everything – but her explanation was so punctuated with sobs and gasps that Aunt Carole only caught the words "biscuit tin" and "trick".

"Trick? What sort of trick?"

"She means a joke," said Alex. "Don't you, Ibby?"

Ibby hesitated. She looked at Alex and then, under his stern gaze, she glanced away again, and nodded meekly.

"I see," said Aunt Carole. She helped Francis to his feet, then picked up the biscuit tin. "Come and have some dinner," she said. "I think we've all had enough tricks for one day. Don't you?"

CHAPTER 4

The Levitation Trick
"WITHOUT THREADS, WIRES OR MAGNETS...!"

Fortunately, Francis seemed none the worse for his ordeal. A little hungrier, perhaps, but that was all. Alex and Ibby observed him closely during dinner, but it wasn't until they were back upstairs again that they were able to question him properly.

"How did you do it?" asked Alex.

"I didn't mean to," said Francis. "I was trying to shrink my inflatable crocodile." He said he'd tapped it three times with the wand, then felt a strange sinking sensation. That was the last thing he remembered before waking up to find himself falling down the stairs.

"So what went wrong?" said Alex.

"I don't know," said Francis. "I did what it said in the book." The only thing he could think of was that perhaps he had been holding the wand the wrong way round – therefore pointing the trick at himself instead of the crocodile. Since the two ends of the wand were so similar (one of the white tips was slightly longer than the other) it was easily done.

"Well, you're lucky we didn't step on you," said Ibby. "Isn't he, Alex?"

But Alex was more interested in the magic set. "Where did you find it?" he asked.

"In the attic," said Francis.

"The attic?" said Alex, surprised. The attic was out of bounds. Aunt Carole said that this was because there wasn't a proper floor – just foam chips between the joists – and that if you stepped in the wrong place your foot could go through the ceiling.

"Does Mum know?"

Francis shook his head. He told them how Aunt Carole had gone up there that morning to get the slide projector for Ibby's mother, and had left the ladder down. He had climbed up afterwards and found the magic set at the back of the attic, in a cardboard box marked "GODFREY".

"Uncle Godfrey!" cried the others.

"Who?"

"The man in the black top hat," said Alex. "The one in the photo."

"What photo?"

"The one on the dresser downstairs."

"Oh, him," said Francis vaguely.

Their Uncle Godfrey had been a professional magician. He had disappeared several years ago in mysterious circumstances. Francis had only been two at the time, so he couldn't remember his uncle at all – but Ibby remembered a tall man in a black top hat, with limp wrists and long, slender fingers, perfect for performing fiddly magic tricks. One Christmas he had startled Ibby by reaching behind her ear and producing a coin. When Ibby had asked him how the trick was done, he had winked at her and said, "Magic!" and Ibby's mother had said, "Don't tease, Godfrey. It's sleight of hand and false bottoms, Ibby – that's all."

But could her mother have been mistaken? Could Uncle Godfrey have been a real magician after all?

Francis picked up the instruction booklet. "What's 'levitation'?" he asked.

"Floating," said Alex. "We'll do that one next."

"Next?" cried Ibby. "You aren't going to do another one, are you?"

"Of course we are," said Alex. "Aren't we, Francis?" Then the two of them went through the rest of the booklet, arguing excitedly.

Ibby frowned. She didn't like the sound of this at all. But fortunately, before the boys could start another trick, Aunt Carole called up the stairs to remind them it was Saturday.

"What's Saturday?" asked Ibby.

"Bath night," said Francis, gloomily.

"Never mind," said Alex, packing up the magic set. "We'll try it again in the morning."

That night, Ibby didn't sleep well. She dreamed that she was lying in a long black box, like a coffin, with her head sticking out one end.

An audience was cheering and applauding, and when Ibby looked round she saw a tall man in a black top hat and satin cloak approaching with a saw.

No good was going to come of this magic set, she was sure of it.

Things often look different in the morning, however. The sun shining through her curtains filled Ibby's bedroom with a yellow light, and for a moment she didn't know where she was. Then she looked around and saw the sloping ceiling and the wardrobe full of jangly wire hangers, and it all came back to her in a rush: Aunt Carole's house, the magic set, and Francis running round and round inside the biscuit tin.

Ibby lay still for a moment, listening to Aunt Carole moving about downstairs. Then she jumped out of bed, put on her dressing gown and rabbit slippers and padded down the corridor to Francis's room. It was empty. Perhaps he was already downstairs having breakfast? But when Ibby got to the kitchen she found that Alex and Francis had already been and gone. Only Aunt Carole was there, in her dressing gown, clearing away their breakfast things.

"Good morning," said Aunt Carole. "Did you sleep well?"

"Yes, thanks," said Ibby.

"Would you like a boiled egg?"

"Yes, please."

Aunt Carole set a brown boiled egg in front of Ibby, then sat down opposite, warming her hands round a mug of tea. While Ibby cut toast fingers for dipping in her yolk, Aunt Carole told her that it had rained during the night but it was going to be a lovely day, and that Ibby could help her pick the last of the raspberries, if she liked.

Ibby nodded absently. In Aunt Carole's kitchen, with Francis's school paintings on the fridge, and jars of cress sprouting on the windowsill, everything seemed so ordinary, so unmagic. It was hard to believe that Francis had really shrunk himself. And yet …

"Aunt Carole," said Ibby cautiously. "Do you believe in magic?"

Aunt Carole, who had just taken a sip of tea, spluttered and choked. She put her mug down suddenly and pushed her chair back.

"Are you all right?" said Ibby.

Aunt Carole was unable to reply. She had

gone very red and was bent double, coughing. Ibby's question seemed to have taken her by surprise.

Ibby jumped out of her chair and thumped Aunt Carole on the back. Gradually Aunt Carole's coughs subsided and her face returned to normal. "Phew!" she said. She took a deep breath, and was just about to speak again when there came a heavy thud from above, which made the ceiling shake. Both Aunt Carole and Ibby glanced upwards. "Goodness me," said Aunt Carole. "What are those two doing now?"

The thud was followed by muffled shouts, laughter, and a crash. What was going on up there?

"I'd better go and see," said Ibby anxiously.

"Aren't you going to finish your egg?"

"No, thanks!" And before Aunt Carole could protest, Ibby had hurried out the door and up the stairs.

Alex had his own room at the end of the corridor. There was a sign on his door that said KEEP OUT and from within there came shouts and laughter. Ibby knocked loudly. The laughter stopped. There was lots of whispering. Then, in a loud voice, Francis said, "Who's there?"

"It's me," said Ibby.

The door opened a crack and Francis looked out. He was wearing the top hat and the cloak. "Are you alone?" he said.

"Of course I'm alone."

The door opened just enough to allow Ibby through. "What's going on?" she said. "What are you—" She stopped in astonishment. Bobbing gently just below the ceiling was Alex.

"He's levitating," said Francis proudly.

"I can see that," said Ibby. Alex was floating just below the ceiling in his dressing gown. His face was flushed with triumph and his hair was flopping forwards.

"Watch!" he said, and he pushed off against the ceiling and went swooping over their heads.

"Careful!" said Ibby, ducking.

"And look!" said Alex. "I can do somersaults, too!" He pushed off again into a forward roll, and his slipper knocked against the lampshade and sent a pattern of light careering round the walls.

"Stop it!" said Ibby crossly. "You're going to break something."

"No, I'm not," said Alex. He shot across the room, crashing into the shelving unit on the opposite wall and sending his swimming trophies and his collection of Napoleonic figurines thudding to the floor.

"See?" said Ibby. "Now look what you've done."

Alex steadied himself. "You're right," he said. "This room is far too small. I need more space …"

"No! Alex – wait!"

But Alex was already going hand over hand along the shelves towards the open window.

"What are you doing?" cried Ibby. "You can't go out! You'll float away!"

"Francis!" said Alex. "Get my lasso."

Francis hurried to the wardrobe and returned with a coil of rope, and Alex took one end of it and tied it round his waist.

"Don't do it, Alex," begged Ibby. "It isn't safe!"

"Of course it's safe. This is what astronauts do when they repair their ship. You don't see *them* floating away, do you?"

"No, but—"

"Hold the end, Francis," instructed Alex. "And whatever happens, DON'T let go." Then out he went, head first, and when the others looked out, there he was, bobbing at the end of the rope in his dressing gown. "Weh-hay!" he shouted.

Francis gave the rope a tug, and Alex rotated slowly.

"Don't!" said Alex.

Francis tugged the rope again, and Alex turned the other way.

"Cut it OUT!" yelled Alex.

Francis laughed, and was about to give the rope another yank when there came a knock at the door that made him jump.

Ibby turned to Francis in alarm. "It's your mother!"

Francis dithered. If Aunt Carole came in now she would wonder why he was standing at the

window holding the end of a rope. But if he hauled Alex in, she would see him floating on the ceiling. What was he to do?

"Here," he said. "Take this!" And he shoved the end of the rope into Ibby's hands.

"*I* don't want it," cried Ibby. She shoved it back at him and there followed a brief flurry of hands as they passed the end of the rope back and forth between them. And then, somehow, it slithered out across the windowsill and was gone.

When Aunt Carole came into the room she found Francis and Ibby both standing with their backs to the window, wearing fixed smiles. There was no sign of the rope, nor of the black top hat and satin cloak. "Is everything all right?" she asked.

"Fine!" they answered.

"What was all that noise?"

"What noise?" said Francis.

"It sounded like things falling."

"Oh, that was just the trophies."

Aunt Carole looked around suspiciously. "Where's Alex?"

"He's gone out."

"Out? Out where?"

"Just out."

Aunt Carole looked at Francis thoughtfully, then she went to the window and looked out. The children held their breath. But there was nothing unusual down there – just an empty rabbit hutch among the nettles. Aunt Carole brought her head back in and said, "I've made some scones. Come down when you want one, won't you?" And out she went again.

As soon as she had gone, Ibby and Francis looked out of the window. To their dismay, Alex had already risen high above the pine trees and was drifting in a northerly direction with the rope trailing uselessly below him.

"Alex!" yelled Francis, through cupped hands.

Alex gave a faint but furious reply. Then, with his arms and legs paddling pathetically, he disappeared beyond the pines.

Air is thinner than water and therefore much more difficult to swim in, so despite winning his swimming club trophy for the 100 metres, Alex's breaststroke was not proving very effective. Within seconds he had cleared the pine trees, crossed the lane, and found himself drifting over a field of sheep.

"Help!" he yelled.

The sheep raised their heads and scattered in all directions, bleating.

A little further on Alex floated over a spinney of birch trees. Crows took to the air, cawing, as he approached. And now the wind was getting stronger. He was climbing steadily. Soon he could see cars moving along distant roads and, in the distance, the slate-grey rooftops and the tall church steeple of Little Wittering. Beyond was just the hazy blue horizon of the sea.

"Help!" cried Alex.

As he approached Little Wittering, the sounds of the town rose up to greet him: car doors slammed and people called to one another in the street. And chiming out above it all were the church bells, calling people to morning service.

This gave Alex an idea. With the concerted effort of a one-time swimming champion, he struck out towards the steeple. At the top of the spire there was a gilded weathervane in the shape of a cockerel, with the letters N, S, W and E. Alex was lucky; the breeze was with him. As he neared the weathervane he drew up his rope and made a noose at one end. He waited until he was just within reach, then threw it.

The first throw glanced off the letter S.

Alex coiled his lasso and got ready to try again. This was his last chance. If he missed this time there was nothing to stop him drifting onwards, out to sea. But as luck would have it the noose fell neatly over the letter W. Quickly, Alex reeled himself in, hand over hand, and wrapped his arms and legs around the steeple.

"HELP!" he bellowed.

Several miles away, Ibby and Francis were squeezing through a gap in a hedge. Ibby came through first, in her dressing gown and rabbit slippers. Her hair was standing out all around her head. Next came Francis, in his pyjamas and wellington boots. They had climbed over gates, waded through stinging nettles and crossed fields of cows. They staggered out into the lane and looked left, then right. "Where are we?" said Ibby.

Francis didn't know.

"So now what do we do?"

Francis didn't know that either.

Ibby made an exasperated sound. "We'll never find him," she said. "He's probably miles away." She looked at the sky, in which nothing but a couple of seagulls wheeled high up against the underbelly of the clouds. What if Alex floated higher and higher, up to where the air was too thin to breathe? What if he rose out of the Earth's atmosphere altogether and ended up a dried-out husk of a boy, circling Earth for all eternity with the rest of the space junk?

"I knew something like this would happen," said Ibby tearfully, and she sat down on the grass verge with her head in her hands. "I wish you'd waited for me before you started levitating people."

"It's not my fault," said Francis, wiping his boot on the grass.

"Yes, it is! If you hadn't let go of the rope, this would never have happened."

"I didn't let go of it! You did!"

"No, I didn't!"

"Yes, you did."

"No, I didn't!"

They were so busy arguing that they didn't hear the distant drone of an approaching vehicle – and they were still arguing when a small bus with "Coastal Express" written on the side appeared round the corner. On the front of the bus it said: "Little Wittering".

At once they both jumped up and down, waving their arms and shouting, "Stop! Stop!"

The bus pulled up, its doors opened with a sigh, and they jumped in.

"We haven't any money!" announced Francis.

"It's an emergency," said Ibby.

The driver looked at Ibby's wild hair and rabbit slippers, and at Francis (who was hitching up his pyjama bottoms), and said nothing. He pressed a little lever on the ticket machine, which spat out two tickets, then the hydraulic doors hissed shut and Ibby and Francis found themselves bumping along in the Coastal Express towards Little Wittering.

Meanwhile, Alex was trying hard to concentrate on the slates right in front of his nose. Every time he looked down he began to feel dizzy. And he was getting heavier now – he could feel it. As every moment passed he had to hug the steeple a little tighter to keep himself from slipping.

"Help!" he wailed.

But nobody heard him. Inside the church there was a service taking place and the voices of the congregation, lifted in song, drowned out his shouts.

Why had he ever let Francis hold the rope in the first place? He should have known that Francis would mess it up. Francis always messed things up. Alex tried to shift a little higher, and his foot dislodged a slate. It went slithering down the steeple like a tiny toboggan and smashed to smithereens on a gravestone below.

"Help!" yelled Alex.

Inside the church, the hymn had come to an

end. The vicar had taken his place in the pulpit, and a hush had fallen over the congregation.

"That hymn," said the vicar, "reminds us that God is everywhere. He is in our homes, our places of work. He is in this church at this very moment, and if we listen He will speak to us. Now, will everyone please turn to hymn number three twenty-seven: 'Raise Your Eyes to Heaven'."

The vicar waited until the rustling of pages had subsided and was just about to begin when there came a faint cry: "Hello?"

The vicar hesitated, and cast a stern eye over his congregation. Was someone playing the fool? "As I was saying," he said. "'Raise Your Eyes to—'"

"Up here!"

Others heard it this time too. People began to mutter and look around. Were they hearing things, or was a voice from on high speaking to them?

"Can anybody HEAR me?" came the plaintive cry.

This time everyone had heard it. A murmur of voices broke out – then one man near the back stood up. "I hear you!" he shouted.

"I hear you too!" cried a lady at the front.

"And me!" said someone else. And then everyone began talking at once.

"People, people!" cried the vicar. He gave the signal for the organist to start playing, in an attempt to restore order – but then the doors of the church flew open and a lady with a Yorkshire terrier rushed in. "Come quickly!" she shrieked. "There's someone on the steeple!"

It was a miracle that no one was crushed in the hurry to get outside and see Him for themselves. But He wasn't quite what they'd expected.

"Good Lord!" said the vicar, pushing to the front. "It's a boy! And it looks like he's wearing pyjamas!"

CHAPTER 7

What Goes Up Must Come Down

Ibby and Francis were still churning down the narrow lanes in the Coastal Express. It wasn't a very full bus. Near the front were two old ladies in rain hoods and a mother accompanied by a little boy sucking a green lollipop. Ibby and Francis took a seat near the back. They were both peering out of the window, hoping to catch a glimpse of Alex in the sky, when the bus braked suddenly and everyone was flung forwards in their seats.

"What's going on?" asked one of the old ladies.

Up ahead there was a long line of traffic. Horns were honking and people were getting out and going to the front.

"I'll go and have a look," said the driver. So everybody waited while he climbed down and spoke to the driver in front. He returned shortly, shaking his head. "Sorry, folks," he said. "There's an incident in Church Street. You'll have to walk from here."

Ibby groaned. "We'll never find Alex now," she said. But there was nothing they could do except continue their journey on foot. There were a lot of other people walking too, and when they got to the end of the street they saw that a huge crowd had gathered outside the church. A police officer was asking everyone to please stand back.

"Has there been an accident?" said Francis to a lady with a Yorkshire terrier.

"Not yet," said the lady.

And that was when they noticed that everyone was peering up at the church spire. It looked like there was someone up there, clinging to the weathervane. Surely not! It couldn't be – could it?

"It's Alex!" shouted Francis. "He's on the steeple!"

It took them nearly an hour to get Alex down. First, the fire engine came and extended its hydraulic platform – but it couldn't reach anywhere near high enough. Then eight firemen stood in the graveyard with a rubber sheet between them, and shouted at Alex to jump – but Alex refused even to look down. In the end they had to call a helicopter. A cheer went up

as it roared in across the rooftops and hovered above the church with its blades whickering loudly. Then a door opened in the side and a man was lowered on a rope. He touched down next to Alex and clipped him into a harness, and when the helicopter rose again both of them were dangling from the end of the rope. They were reeled back into the helicopter before it swung round and descended in the churchyard, generating a wind that lifted several hats and sent them spinning down the street.

"Hooray!" cried the crowd.

The door opened and out came Alex, draped in a blanket. He was met by a policeman.

"Alex!" yelled Francis cheerfully. "It's us!"

But if Alex heard, he gave no sign.

"Alex!" yelled Francis, waving. "We're here!"

Francis struggled through the crowd with Ibby close behind him and they arrived breathless and smiling just as Alex turned around, pointed straight at Francis and said coldly, "That's him. It's all his fault."

Francis's face fell.

PC Mackenzie looked at Francis in his pyjamas, and at Ibby in her dressing gown, and said, "I think you'd all better get in the car. I'll take you home." So Ibby, Francis and Alex climbed into the back seat, and the police car pulled away with photographers from the *Weekly News* running alongside and taking pictures through the windows.

For a long while nobody spoke. Then Francis said, "Next time, I'll tie you on to something."

"Next time," retorted Alex, "*I'll* be the magician."

"But that's not fair!" protested Francis. "I'm the one who—"

"Boys, boys!" said PC Mackenzie, glancing in the rearview mirror. "That's enough! And let's have no more talk of 'next time'. Understood?"

Alex and Francis both sat back meekly and

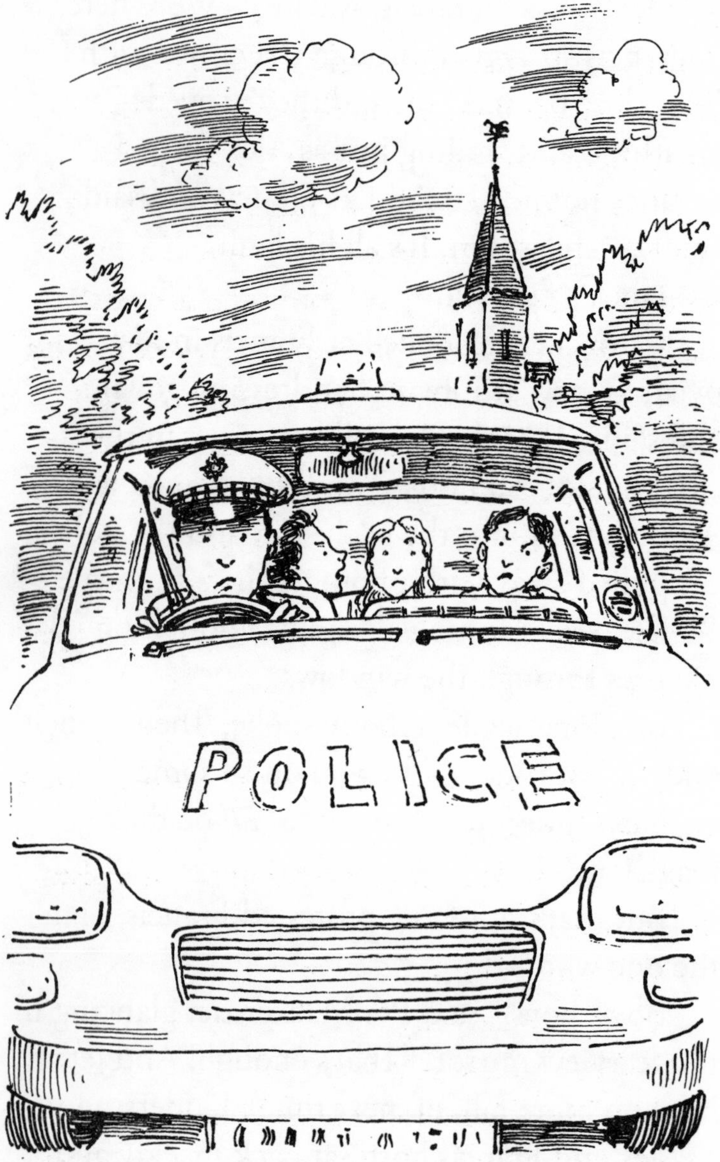
POLICE

didn't say another word all the way home.

Aunt Carole rushed outside when she saw
the police car coming up the drive. "What
happened?" she cried. "Are they all right?"

PC Mackenzie told the children to stay in
the car while he and Aunt Carole had a "talk",
so they all had to sit in gloomy silence while
he and Aunt Carole spoke in low voices on the
front step. Every now and then Aunt Carole
shook her head and shot dark glances in their
direction. And then, eventually, PC Mackenzie
returned to the car and let them all out.

"Thanks again," said Aunt Carole.

"Any time," said PC Mackenzie. Then he got
back in his car and drove away.

"What possessed you?" said Aunt Carole, when
they got inside.

Alex mumbled something that no one else
could hear.

"Pardon?" said Aunt Carole.

"I said it wasn't my fault."

"Whose fault was it then?"

"His," said Alex, looking at Francis.

Francis blinked. He looked small and rather

blameless in his pyjamas and wellington boots.

"I suppose Francis *made* you climb it, did he?" said Aunt Carole.

"I didn't climb it."

"That's not what PC Mackenzie said. He said you were right at the top."

"I was. But I didn't climb up there."

"How did you get up there then? Fly?"

"I can't tell you," said Alex.

Aunt Carole made an exasperated noise. In that case, she said, Alex could go to his room and think long and hard about what he'd done. Alex was furious. If anyone should be thinking long and hard about what they'd done, he said, it should be Francis, and choking back tears he stomped upstairs in his dressing gown. Unfortunately, he still wasn't quite as heavy as he ought to be, so he bounced lightly on each step, giving the impression he was cheerful. To make up for it he slammed his door extra hard so that the KEEP OUT sign fell off.

Poor Alex. Ibby couldn't help feeling sorry for him. It must have been horrible stuck on the steeple in his dressing gown, with everybody looking. And she couldn't help feeling partly responsible – even though she had warned him not to go out of the window. So she went upstairs and knocked timidly on his bedroom door. "Alex?" she said. "It's me. Can I come in?"

"NO!" barked Alex.

So Ibby put the KEEP OUT sign back on the door and crept away again.

CHAPTER 8

The Disappearing Coin

"YOUR AUDIENCE WILL NOT BELIEVE WHAT'S RIGHT IN FRONT OF THEIR EYES."

It is always awkward being in someone else's house when they've been told off. You don't know where to put yourself. Eventually, Ibby went to her room and lay on her bed reading. It is uncomfortable reading in bed though, unless you've got lots of pillows at your back. If you lie on your side you have to support your head with your hand, and after a while your wrist gets stiff. And Ibby couldn't really concentrate knowing that Aunt Carole was cross, and that Alex was probably crying his eyes out in his room. So presently she closed her book and went downstairs. She found Aunt Carole in the kitchen, grating Cheddar to make macaroni cheese.

"Hello," said Aunt Carole cheerfully. "Everything all right?"

"Yes, thanks," said Ibby.

"Not feeling homesick then?"

"No," said Ibby. "Not at all." To her surprise, she realized this was true. So much had happened since yesterday that she hadn't had time to think about missing home. Ibby picked up a crumb of cheese on the end of her finger and ate it. Then she said, "It wasn't his fault, you know."

"What wasn't?"

"Getting stuck on the steeple."

Aunt Carole sighed. "It's kind of you to defend him, Ibby, but Alex is old enough to take responsibility for his actions." The pile of cheese was getting big now, so Aunt Carole tipped it into a casserole dish and carried on grating vigorously.

Ibby tried another approach. "Aunt Carole," she said. "Do you know what 'levitation' is?"

Suddenly Aunt Carole's hand slipped. She gave a cry and examined the end of her finger. There was a red drop of blood beading on the tip.

"Oh!" said Ibby in dismay.

"My fault," said Aunt Carole, putting her finger under the cold tap. "I wasn't concentrating."

Ibby looked on while Aunt Carole dried her

finger on a paper towel and found some plasters in the drawer. Aunt Carole had seemed startled by her question. Was that why her hand had slipped? Or had it just been a coincidence? Before Ibby could find out, she heard feet pounding down the stairs, and Alex and Francis appeared in the doorway.

"When's dinner?" asked Alex. Somewhat to Ibby's irritation, he appeared to have completely recovered from his ordeal.

"Twenty minutes," Aunt Carole said, wrapping a plaster round her finger. "I'll call you when it's ready."

Alex and Francis exchanged a significant look, then ran upstairs again.

"Now – what were you saying?" asked Aunt Carole.

Ibby hesitated. "Nothing," she said, and she turned and hurried out after the others.

Aunt Carole stood and watched her go, thoughtfully.

Ibby found the boys in Francis's room. They had cleared a space on the floor and were sitting round the magic set. "You're not doing another trick now, are you?" she said.

"Yep," said Alex.

"But there isn't time! We're eating in twenty minutes."

This didn't seem to bother Alex. He had already taken the lid off the magic set and was examining the contents.

Set into the plastic tray were several curious items: a hand mirror, a red silk handkerchief, a silver coin, a gold key and a pack of cards. Ibby eyed them all suspiciously.

"What does this do?" asked Francis, fingering the handkerchief.

"That's the Multicoloured Handkerchief," said Alex. "It changes colour each time you pull it out of the hat."

"That sounds all right," said Ibby cautiously. After all, you couldn't do much damage with a handkerchief, could you?

"No, it doesn't," said Alex. "It sounds boring."

But Francis wanted to try it anyway.

"Well, you can't," said Alex.

"Yes, I can!" shouted Francis, and he went on to say that no one ever did what he wanted, and that since he was the one who had found the magic set in the first place, he should be allowed to do all the magic tricks. Then his mouth turned down at the corners and his chin began to tremble.

"Oh, all right," said Alex wearily. "But the next trick is mine."

Francis cheered up instantly. He shook out the black satin cloak and put it round his shoulders. Then, following the instructions carefully, he put the handkerchief into the top hat and recited the following lines:

> A hanky sits
> Within this hat
> It went in red
> And comes out - black!

He stirred the air three times with the magic wand. The handkerchief started swirling round and round inside the hat, like water going down a plughole. As it went round, it turned darker and darker – and by the time it had stopped swirling, it was black! Delighted, Francis turned it blue next, and then pink – and it worked well until Ibby said "Taupe" and then it went a muddy sort of colour and refused to change again.

"Now look what you've done," said Alex.

Francis folded the handkerchief carefully and put it back. Perhaps it would be all right again after a rest.

"What about the key?" said Ibby hastily. "What does that do?" Unlike the other props, which fitted snugly into plastic hollows, the key lay in an oval depression that seemed far too large for it.

"That's the key from the Vanishing Act," said Alex. "You get a box and lock something inside it, then when you open the box again, the object has vanished. You have to do the trick again to get it back."

"Let's try it with your watch!" cried Francis.

But Alex wouldn't. His watch was a large black digital with lots of buttons and he didn't want to risk it. "Anyway," he said. "It wouldn't work. The padlock is missing."

Francis checked under the plastic tray. There was no padlock, but as he tipped the tray, the silver coin fell out and rolled onto the carpet. Alex picked it up and looked at it. On one side there was the head of a man in a top hat. On the other side there was nothing. "It's the Disappearing Coin," he said.

"What does it do?" asked Francis.

"Disappears, duh," said Alex rudely.

Under the Disappearing Coin trick there was a series of tiny diagrams of a magician making movements with his right arm as though directing traffic. He was balancing the coin on his right elbow, then catching it with his right hand.

"Easy-peasy," said Alex. He put the coin on his elbow, then brought his hand round, quick, to catch it – but the coin flew off and hit the carpet with a thud.

Francis sniggered.

"Stand up and do it," suggested Ibby. So Alex stood up and put the coin back on his elbow. But this time the coin flew across the room and struck the opposite wall.

"Can I have a go?" asked Francis.

Alex ignored him. He retrieved the coin and tried again and again, getting more and more annoyed with each attempt. Eventually he gave up. "I don't think it's possible," he said, putting the coin back in the tray.

"What about the cards?" said Ibby.

Alex brightened. "I'm good at cards."

While Alex was getting them out of their packet Francis stole another look at the

instruction booklet. It was lying open at the Disappearing Coin trick. There was a short rhyme on the facing page. Francis recited it softly to himself:

> Watch me very closely,
> See how it's done.
> Now you see me.
> Now I'm GONE!

He took the coin out of the tray, bent his right arm like the man in the diagram, and balanced the coin on his elbow. Then he brought his hand forwards quickly, to catch it. But the coin dropped off and rolled across the carpet. Francis tried again. He was closer the second time. The trick, he thought, was to bring your elbow backwards at the same time as you brought your hand forwards. So, while Alex was showing Ibby how to shuffle, Francis went back and forth in the black top hat and satin cloak, balancing the coin on his elbow, lunging forwards, missing, and then trying again. And then all of a sudden, he caught it! He let out a whoop of surprise. "Did you see that?"

"See what?" said Ibby, looking round.

"I caught it! I caught the Disappearing Coin!"
There was a shocked pause.

"You needn't look so surprised," said Francis.

The others remained silent. They were still
staring at the place where Francis's voice was
coming from. Francis – and the coin – had
completely disappeared.

"What's the matter?" said Francis. There was
a note of doubt in his voice now. "What are you
staring at?"

"Nothing," said Ibby eventually. "Absolutely
nothing at all."

CHAPTER 9

Francis Disappears

Alex crossed the room with his arms outstretched, like someone playing blindman's bluff without the blindfold.

"What are you doing?" Francis's voice sounded as though it had moved a little to the left. "What are you – ouch!"

"He's here!" reported Alex. "I can feel him."

"Of course I'm here," said Francis.

"But, Francis," wailed Ibby, "you're not."

"What do you mean?" said Francis uncertainly.

"Look at yourself! You've disappeared."

The others heard Francis's footsteps move across the room and stop in front of the mirror. There was a pause, then they saw his breath fog up the glass. A moment later, one of his dresser drawers seemed to open and close of its own accord. "It's true!" came his voice. "I'm invisible!" His footsteps moved back across the room and the others followed his progress by the objects which appeared to leap into the air of their own volition. Then all of a sudden Alex gave a yell and clapped his hand to his ear. "Ow!"

Francis giggled.

"All right, Francis, that's enough," said Alex crossly. "Give me the coin."

Francis was silent.

"Francis?" said Alex.

There was a pause, then Francis spoke again – from the other side of the room, this time. "No!" he said.

"Right!" said Alex, advancing with his arms outstretched. Francis could be heard laughing and running away – then the bedsprings creaked.

"Ha!" said Alex, flinging himself on the bed.

Ibby heard Francis give a disembodied shriek, then the struggle began. It was strangely disconcerting to watch since it looked as though Alex was having a fit. He staggered round the room, stumbling over toys and hurling himself into walls with a terrible expression on his face.

"Stop it!" cried Ibby. "Just stop it!"

She did her best to come between them, but it's hard to separate two fighting people

– especially when one of them is invisible. Fortunately, the fight was interrupted by Aunt Carole calling up the stairs, "Dinner's ready!"

Alex fell back, panting. "You'll have to come back now!" he said.

But Francis was stubbornly quiet.

"Please come back, Francis," said Ibby. "You can't let Aunt Carole see you like this, can you?"

Francis remained silent.

"Mmm – it's macaroni cheese," said Alex slyly. Macaroni cheese was Francis's favourite. Alex opened the bedroom door and wafted it back and forth a few times, bringing the cheesy smell into the room.

"All right," said Francis suddenly. "What do I have to do?"

"You've got to catch the coin again," said Ibby. "But be careful." (She had noticed that beside this particular step Uncle Godfrey had scribbled: 243 attempts!!!) "Do it over there, near the wall. If you drop it now, we'll never—"

But it was too late. They heard a rattling among the pile of board games and jigsaw boxes. It sounded just like something small getting lost among them.

Alex groaned.

"It's all right," said Francis. "It's here somewhere." And the games began shifting left and right as Francis rooted through them. Alex and Ibby went to help. They ran their hands over the carpet, but all they found was an old penny, a limpet shell and a button – no invisible coin.

"We'll have to search the whole room now," said Alex.

They surveyed the room despondently. Francis had a lot of toys, and every single one of them was lying on the floor. Aunt Carole was always telling Francis to tidy his room, but he never did. It was littered with stuffed toys, building blocks and plastic figures; the invisible coin could be anywhere. Then Ibby had a bright idea. "Do you still have your metal detector?"

"Yes!" cried Alex. He ran to his room and returned a minute later with what looked like a lightweight vacuum cleaner. But before they could begin the search, Aunt Carole shouted up the stairs again, "IT'S GOING COLD!"

Alex passed the metal detector to Francis. "You'll have to stay up here," he said, "until you find it."

"But what about my macaroni cheese?"

Alex shrugged. "The quicker you find the coin, the quicker you can come downstairs."

"That's not fair!"

"Neither was doing the coin trick when it wasn't your turn," said Alex, and he turned on his heel and marched out the door.

"Don't worry, Francis," said Ibby to an apparently empty room. "We'll help you look when we get back." Then she went out too, and closed the door behind her, leaving Francis standing lonely and invisible amid the sea of scattered toys.

"Where's Francis?" asked Aunt Carole.

"He's not hungry," said Alex.

"Not hungry?" This was a surprise. Aunt Carole had never known Francis not to be hungry before – and especially not when they were having macaroni cheese. "Is he feeling all right?"

"Yes," said Alex, sitting down. "He's fine."

Aunt Carole regarded Alex doubtfully. "I think I'd better go and check."

"No!" cried Alex, jumping up again. "You mustn't!"

But Aunt Carole had already started up the stairs. Alex and Ibby looked at one another in alarm, then hurried after her.

Francis's bedroom door was closed, and from within there came the faint hum of the metal detector. "Francis?" said Aunt Carole. "Are you all right?"

Immediately the metal detector stopped and they heard the thud of running feet, then the squeak of bedsprings. Then silence. Aunt Carole opened the door and went in. The curtains were drawn and there was a long sausage-shaped lump in Francis's bed. "Francis?" she said. "What are you doing? It's only six o'clock."

From under the duvet there came a muffled

reply.

"I can't hear you," said Aunt Carole. "Sit up."

The sausage-shaped lump didn't move.

"Francis!" said Aunt Carole sternly. "Sit up this minute, and let me look at you."

"No!"

"Why not?"

"Because you can't!"

"Oh – don't make him, Aunt Carole!" cried Ibby. "He's not ... his usual self."

Aunt Carole looked at Ibby in surprise. "Why? What's the matter with him?"

Ibby hesitated. She was not a liar, and it would have been a relief to tell her aunt

everything then – about the magic set and about how Francis had shrunk himself, and about how Alex had never meant to end up on the steeple. But before she could tell the truth, Alex said, "He's sulking."

"Sulking?" Aunt Carole looked confused. "Why is he sulking?"

Alex shrugged.

Aunt Carole addressed the lump sternly. "Is this true, Francis? Are you sulking?"

"No!" said Francis miserably.

"What's the matter then?"

"Nothing!"

"Well!" said Aunt Carole, exasperated. "In that case, perhaps you'd better stay up here until you're in a better mood. Come on, the rest of you – out!"

So out they all went.

As soon as the door had closed, however, Francis's duvet was flung back. The indentation in the mattress lifted, and a moment later his bottom drawer yanked open and a bundle of sweaters lifted out and arranged themselves in the bed. Next, Francis's football rose off the floor, crossed the room and nestled into the pillow. Then the duvet folded back over everything and tucked itself in. Finally, Francis's footsteps retreated, the door opened and closed, and the room was still again.

Francis stood on the landing for a moment, listening. Downstairs, he could hear the clink of cutlery and the murmur of conversation. It wasn't fair, he thought. Why should he have to stay in his room looking for the coin while everyone else was downstairs eating macaroni cheese? He got the blame for everything! Well – now he would show them. He would run away. Then they'd all be sorry.

Quietly, Francis tiptoed down the stairs and along the hall and peered round the kitchen door. Unexpectedly, Aunt Carole glanced up. Perhaps she had heard a tread on the stairs, or perhaps she felt Francis's invisible eyes upon her. But although she seemed to look straight at him, her face didn't change at all.

Francis stiffened. It was horrible being looked at like that by his own mother – it was as though she didn't know him. Francis smothered a sob. Then he ran down the hall, opened the front door, and stepped outside.

CHAPTER 10

The Ferris Wheel Ghost

"BEFORE YOU KNOW IT YOU'LL BE PERFORMING PROFESSIONAL MAGIC TRICKS THAT WILL BAFFLE AUDIENCES OF ALL AGES."

Had Aunt Carole been looking out of the kitchen window just then, she might have seen Francis's bike pick itself up off the ground. She might have seen its pedals start turning, all by themselves. And she might even have heard the trill of its bell as it disappeared down the drive.

But she didn't. None of them did.

As Francis pedalled further from the house, the tightness in his heart lifted and turned into excitement. He had never been out on his own in the evening before. A little way down the lane

79

a Jack Russell shot out of a driveway, barking, and chased after the bike. But when the dog noticed that the bike was riderless, it stopped in the middle of the road with its head cocked and one ear up.

Francis laughed at its puzzled face, and pedalled on.

The lane was quiet. Francis could hear birds singing in the hedges, and sheep bleating in the fields. Then, carried on the wind came snatches of hurdy-gurdy music and the smell of popcorn, and as Francis turned the corner there it was, in the field opposite Billington's Garage – the funfair!

When the others got back upstairs they found that the curtains were closed, the room was dim, and the lump in Francis's bed still hadn't moved.

"Well?" said Alex, prodding the lump. "Have you found it yet?"

The sausage-shaped lump made no reply.

"Come on, Francis," said Ibby kindly. "We'll help you look."

The lump was silent.

"I don't know why he's being like this," said Alex crossly. "He's only got himself to blame."

Ibby sighed. She couldn't help feeling sorry for Francis. He hadn't meant to lose the Disappearing Coin – and it must be horrible knowing that no one could see you. She sat on the edge of the bed and patted the lump's back. "Don't worry, Francis," she said. "It's bound to wear off eventually."

But the lump remained unmoved.

"Ignore him," said Alex. "We'll find the coin ourselves." So Ibby turned on the light and Alex switched on the metal detector, and they had just begun beeping systematically across the carpet when Aunt Carole came up and asked them what they were doing making all this noise while Francis was trying to sleep. So, much to Alex's annoyance, they had to switch off the detector, put out the light, and leave the lump in silence.

"Good night, Francis," whispered Ibby.

From the lump there was no reply.

Francis, meanwhile, was making the most of being invisible. First, he had walked straight past the ticket kiosk and gone into the fair without paying. Then he had climbed onto one of the horses on the merry-go-round and enjoyed three turns before another boy chose to ride the same horse, which meant that Francis had to jump off quickly. Next (since he hadn't had any dinner) Francis wandered round the fairground tearing bits off people's candyfloss and stealing licks from ice creams. (One little girl watched, speechless, as several bits of popcorn rose out of her container and disappeared in mid-air.) After that, Francis spent a satisfying half-hour in the haunted house, shouting "BOO!" into people's ears, and by the time he emerged it was getting dark. The fairground rides were all lit up and flashing like Christmas trees. And there it was – the best ride of all – towering high above the fairground against a starry sky: the Ferris wheel.

Francis ducked under the barrier and scrambled into an empty carriage. He had only just put the bar down before the wheel began turning. Up, up, up he went, until he could see the whole fairground spread out below – and beyond, to the twinkling lights of distant towns. Then down, down, down again, back among the heady smells of popcorn and fried onions.

Every time the ride ended, Francis stayed put. And when the next passengers tried to climb into his carriage, he leaned on the bar so they couldn't lift it up. Eventually the operators put a sign on his carriage that said: OUT OF ORDER.

Francis sighed happily. It was wonderful being invisible. He could ride the Ferris wheel all night. And think of all the other things he could do: he could follow Alex and his friends around without them even knowing he was there; he could creep downstairs and watch television with his mother when he was supposed to be in bed – and, best of all, he need never wash his face or brush his hair again!

It was while he was thinking these happy thoughts that Francis realized the Ferris wheel had stopped. One by one the carriages had emptied, and when Francis looked down he saw the last couple climbing out. People were making their way to the exit. The popcorn seller was packing up. Then the operators flicked a switch and all the lights on the Ferris wheel went out.

"Hey!" yelled Francis, rattling the bar.

But nobody heard him. His cries were drowned out by shouts of "Good night!" and "See you tomorrow!" Doors slammed and engines revved and vans bumped out through

the gate. Sooner than you'd expect, the fairground was deserted, leaving only silent rides and a field littered with popcorn containers and empty wrappers. And above it all rose a plaintive wail: "I want to go home!"

It can get cold at the top of a Ferris wheel at night – and windy too – and you get just as cold when you're invisible as you do when everyone can see you. Colder, even. The wind grew stronger and the frame of the Ferris wheel shuddered. Francis considered getting out and climbing down, but with one leg over the side of his carriage, the ground looked a long way away. He put his leg back in again. And then it began to rain. It came in gusts, flinging itself against the sides of the carriage like grit. Francis huddled in one corner of the seat with his cheek pressed against the wet vinyl and the raindrops mingling with his tears – and for the first time in his life, he knew what it was like to feel truly invisible.

But morning always comes. Finally, the rain stopped and the sky began to pale low down over the horizon. Gradually it got brighter and brighter. Cars started moving on distant roads, the first starling began to sing and then, like a fanfare, a blinding sun appeared. And Francis knew that the worst was over.

It was a jogger who raised the alarm. As she was passing the fairground gate she heard a faint cry: "Up here!" It sounded as though it was coming from the top of the Ferris wheel – and to confirm it, one of the uppermost carriages was rocking impatiently.

"Hold on!" she called through cupped hands. "Help is on the way!"

Soon the police arrived, and the fairground workers too, and they started the Ferris wheel turning. But it was most mysterious; when the uppermost carriages descended, they were seen to be unoccupied. No one could figure it out. The Ferris wheel operators were convinced it was a ghost.

Of course, what had really happened was that as soon as his carriage had come down, the invisible Francis had climbed stiffly out, hurried back to his bike, and cycled home. He found the front door locked and the house quiet, so he put a ladder up against the wall and climbed back in through his bedroom window. Then he changed into his pyjamas and fell, exhausted, into bed.

When Francis didn't come down for breakfast his mother went upstairs and found him sound asleep. "Wake up, sleepy-head!" she said.

Francis sat up – and saw his mother smiling fondly at him, just as usual. "Mum?" he said. "Can you see me?"

"Silly sausage! Of course I can see you!" said Aunt Carole. "And what's that all around your mouth? It looks like toothpaste."

"It's ice cream," said Francis, tasting it.

Aunt Carole laughed. "Get dressed, silly," she said. "I've got a special treat for you today. We're going to the fair!"

They never did find the Disappearing Coin. They found plenty of other things: a pen lid, a doll's arm, a missing piece from one of Francis's jigsaws. But no coin. Alex was furious. He had been looking forward to sneaking invisibly into the nine-screen cinema in Greater Wittering and spending whole weekends in there, wandering from film to film and living on popcorn and fizzy drinks after everyone else had gone home.

"From now on," he said. "I do the tricks alone."

"That's not fair!" protested Francis.

"Tough," said Alex, and he took the magic set and marched back to his room. Francis hurried after him, protesting, and hammered on the door until Aunt Carole came upstairs and told him to leave his brother alone.

Alex remained in his room for the rest of the morning. From time to time Ibby and Francis went and put their ears to the door – but all was strangely quiet. Ibby thought that every now and again she heard a page turn, but Francis thought it sounded more like cards being shuffled.

"What are you doing in there?" he shouted.

There was no reply.

Alex emerged at lunchtime. He looked smug and secretive, but when Francis asked him what he had been doing, he just tapped the side of his nose in an irritating manner and said, "All in good time."

Then, that afternoon, Aunt Carole went out. "I'm going to town to do the food shop," she said. "Will you be all right on your own?"

They all assured her that they would.

"Oh! And I nearly forgot. I'm expecting a delivery today. Some geraniums. Ask the man to put them in the kitchen, would you, Alex?"

Alex said he would.

"Be good then, everyone," said Aunt Carole. And out she went, slamming the door behind her.

The moment she had gone, Alex said, "Right!" and ran upstairs.

Ibby and Francis both jumped up and hurried after him. "You aren't going to do anything silly, are you?" said Ibby.

Alex just grinned. He went straight to his room and put on the black top hat and satin cloak. "Ladies and gentlemen," he said. "Prepare to be astonished! Prepare to be amazed! Before your very eyes I will be transformed!"

"Transformed?" said Ibby anxiously. "Transformed into what?"

"Myself. But older."

Francis looked perplexed. "Older?"

"Yes." Alex opened the instruction booklet at a place marked with a leather bookmark. At the top of the page it said The Life Cycle. Most of the page was taken up by a large circle broken at intervals by little illustrations. It looked a lot like the life cycle of the frog that you find in biology books at school – only here, instead of frog spawn and tadpoles, the pictures were of people. At the top of the circle was a baby with a nappy on. At the three o'clock position were a boy and a girl standing hand in hand with no clothes on. At the bottom of the circle were a man and a woman wearing fig leaves, and at the nine o'clock position was a bent old couple

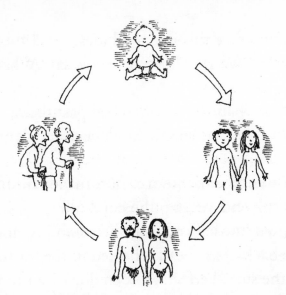

leaning on sticks.

"I'm here," said Alex, pointing to the boy and the girl holding hands. "And when I do the trick, I advance one stage forward, to here." And he pointed at the man and the woman wearing fig leaves.

"You want to grow up?" said Francis doubtfully.

Alex took the hand mirror out of the magic set. "It's all done with mirrors," he explained. "You've got to say the magic words while looking at the back of your head – that's why they give you the hand mirror. Then when you look at your face again you see that you've moved into the next stage of the Life Cycle."

"Are you sure this is a good idea?" said Ibby nervously. "What will Aunt Carole say? What if—"

But Alex had already marched past them, gone into the bathroom, and locked the door.

Once inside the bathroom, Alex turned his back to the sink and held up the hand mirror. If he positioned himself correctly, he could just about see the back of his head reflected in the mirror above the sink. Perfect! Alex couldn't wait to be an adult. When you were an adult you didn't have your little brother following you around, did you? And you didn't have your mother telling you what to do either. When you were an adult you could go wherever you liked and do whatever you wanted. Perhaps he'd become a professional magician, like his Uncle Godfrey. Just think – he might become famous!

Alex considered his reflection thoughtfully. If he was going to be on television he had better smarten himself up a little.

Outside, Ibby and Francis had their ears to the bathroom door. They heard the cabinet above the sink open and close. Then they heard the hiss of deodorant spray, and the scuff of someone brushing their hair.

"What are you doing?" called Francis.

There was no reply. Presently they heard muttering, and a little while later there was a hoarse yell and the sound of something clattering to the floor.

"Are you all right?" cried Ibby.

Next, they heard a tap running and water splashing in the sink, and what sounded like someone's cheeks being slapped. A heady scent came wafting under the door.

"Let us in!" yelled Francis, rattling the handle.

"Good grief!" said an unexpectedly deep voice. "Can't a fellow get a minute's peace?" Then the bolt went back, the door flew open – and there stood a tall, slim, moustached man whom neither of them had ever seen before.

"Alex?" they said.

"Well?" said the man-who-had-been-Alex. "What do you think?"

There was an uncomfortable silence. The truth was, if it hadn't been for the top hat and the satin cloak they would never have recognized him. His face was longer and thinner than it had been, and on his upper lip he wore a

bristly little moustache. He was taller too. His sweatshirt exposed a wide expanse of midriff, and his jeans looked uncomfortably tight.

"Well?" said Alex, pushing up his sleeves.

Ibby hesitated. "You're very ..." She searched for the right words. "Very ..."

"Old," said Francis, awed.

The man-who-had-been-Alex frowned. "Old?" he said. "I'm not old! I'm in the prime of life!" And he made an irritated sound and marched back to his room. The others watched from the doorway as he pulled a flattened rucksack out from the bottom of his wardrobe, then began going round the room stuffing things into it.

"What are you doing?" said Francis.

"Packing," said Alex.

"Packing? Why? Where are you going?"

"Out-into-the-world," said Alex grandly. "To seek my fortune."

Francis's face lit up. "Can I come too?"

"No."

"Why not?"

"Because you can't!"

Francis watched, crestfallen, as Alex stuffed pyjamas, a fistful of socks and several pairs of underwear into his rucksack. It looked as though he intended to be away for quite some time.

"But what will we tell Aunt Carole?" said Ibby in distress.

"Who?"

"Your mother!"

"Oh – her. Tell her I'll send her a postcard." After a moment's hesitation, Alex packed his biggest swimming trophy, a survival handbook, and a waterproof coat that stuffed into its own pocket.

"But how will you live?" persisted Ibby. "What will you do about money?"

"I'm taking my metal detector. Money always falls out of people's pockets on the beach – and in the park."

Ibby looked at Francis helplessly. It seemed that Alex had thought of everything – or nearly everything. "Food!" said Alex suddenly. He threw his rucksack over his shoulder, picked up his metal detector and marched out of the room.

CHAPTER 12

The Intruder

"YOUR OWN MOTHER WOULDN'T RECOGNIZE YOU."

It just so happened that at that very moment the van from Gardens on the Move was pulling up outside. Out jumped the delivery man wearing blue overalls and a baseball cap. He made a note on his clipboard, got Aunt Carole's box of geraniums out of the back of his van, and was just heading up the garden path when he heard raised voices. He paused. The voices were coming through the open kitchen window. One of the voices belonged to a girl.

"Aunt Carole will be back in a minute!" said the girl. "She'll stop you!"

"No, she won't," answered a young man. "She'll not be back until three o'clock. I'll be long gone by then."

"She'll call the police!" said the girl. "They'll send out a search party!"

The young man laughed. "How will they find me? They don't even know what I look like!"

The delivery man drew in his breath sharply.

He knew trouble when he heard it. He hurried up the path and peered in through the kitchen window, and to his alarm he saw a man wearing a black top hat and satin cloak. The man was going round the kitchen opening cupboards and drawers and helping himself to the contents. Into his bag went a jar of peanut butter, an unopened packet of ginger biscuits, an apple and the salt shaker. The delivery man gasped. A burglary was taking place – and two brave children were trying to prevent it!

With trembling hands the delivery man fished his phone out of his overalls pocket and dialled. "Police?" he said. "Come quickly! I'm witnessing

a burglary!" He gave Aunt Carole's address, then peered back in through the kitchen window. To his horror he saw the cloaked intruder open the cutlery drawer, take out a cheese knife and test the blade with his thumb.

"Hey!" yelled the delivery man, banging loudly on the window.

Instantly, all three faces looked around – and each looked equally alarmed. For a moment nobody moved. Then Alex dropped the knife and fled.

The delivery man ran up the front steps and burst in through the front door just in time to see Alex flying up the stairs two at a time, with his cloak billowing out behind him.

"That's right!" shouted the delivery man. "Run away!" And he hurried upstairs after Alex, followed closely by Ibby and Francis. But he was too late. Alex had already ducked into the bathroom, slammed the door and shot the bolt.

Of course, Ibby and Francis tried to tell the delivery man that it was all a mistake – but it was no use. He was only half listening. Every now and again Alex opened the bathroom door a crack and tried to explain, but the delivery man flapped his clipboard at the gap and the door slammed shut again. "Don't panic, kids," he kept saying. "The police are on their way."

So there was nothing they could do but wait – and they didn't have to wait long. Within minutes there were voices in the hall, and DI Davies and a lady officer called PC Preston came charging up the stairs.

"He's in here!" said the delivery man.

DI Davies stepped up close and put his ear to the door. "We know you're in there," he said sternly. "Come out with your hands up."

From the bathroom there was no reply.

"I'm going to count to five," said DI Davies. "And if you don't come out on the count of five, we're coming in to get you." He took his baton out, and PC Preston did the same.

"One …" said DI Davies.

From the bathroom there came the sound of cupboard doors opening and closing.

"Two …"

There was muttering within.

"Three – I'm warning you! Four …"

And then, just as DI Davies put his shoulder to the door, the bolt went back, the door opened, and there stood …

An old man.

The others gasped. The old man's eyes were
tired and droopy like the eyes of a basset hound,
and he had a long white beard and moustache.
If it hadn't been for the fact that he was still
wearing the top hat and the satin cloak, the
others would never have recognized him.

"But … but … that's not him!" spluttered the delivery man. "It was a younger man. I'm sure of it!"

"I am a younger man," said Alex hoarsely. He took a few steps forward, staggered and clutched at PC Preston's shoulder for support.

"There must be someone else in there," said the delivery man, and he ran into the bathroom and could be heard opening the cupboards and drawing back the shower curtain. But of course the bathroom was empty.

"Have either of you children seen this man before?" asked PC Preston.

The children had to admit that they hadn't.

"Where do you live, sir?" said DI Davies to the man-who-had-been-Alex.

Alex pointed a crooked finger and tried to head off down the corridor. But PC Preston took him by the arm. "Not so fast, sir," she said. "I think you'd better come with us. We'll see you home again."

Alex protested weakly, but the officers ignored him.

"Where are you taking him?" cried Ibby.

"Back to the station," said PC Preston. "To check the Missing Persons Database. I expect he lost his way. It's not unusual."

"Oh! Can't we keep him here?" said Francis. "Just until the morning?"

"Yes," said Ibby. "Things might look quite different then."

"That's kind of you," said PC Preston. "But the sooner we get him home, the better, don't you think?"

Ibby nodded meekly. There was nothing else to say. She and Francis could only watch in dismay as the police officers helped Alex down the stairs and into the back of their car. The last thing that the children saw as it drove away was Alex's mournful face, mouthing a silent protest through the rear window.

Alex couldn't understand what had gone wrong. He'd assumed that if he did the trick again he would revert back to his former self – but instead he had moved forwards into the last phase of the Life Cycle. If only he had read the instructions properly! He had to get back and consult the instruction booklet. It was his only hope.

Alex leaned forwards and knocked on the glass partition, but the officers ignored him. He rattled the door handle, but it was locked. Then he had an idea. He noticed that if he shuffled sideways a little, he could catch a glimpse of his reflection in the rear-view mirror – and he still had the hand mirror in his pocket. Why not try the trick again? He was in the last stage of the Life Cycle now, so he couldn't go any further, could he? Certainly things couldn't get any worse. Perhaps it was only when the cycle was finished that he would return to normal.

If Alex turned around and held up the hand mirror, he could just about make out the back of his head in the rear-view mirror. It wasn't easy. Every time the car went round a bend or over a bump, he lost sight of his reflection. But he had better hurry. Soon they would be at Little Wittering police station.

"Ladies and gentlemen …" he began.

Back at Aunt Carole's house, the delivery man had driven off again, and Ibby and Francis were sitting at the kitchen table wondering how they were going to explain Alex's disappearance.

"If he's still got the mirror," said Francis, "he can turn himself back again, can't he?"

"I don't think you can go backwards," said Ibby. "You can only go forwards."

"What if he goes forwards then?"

"He's already in Phase Four," said Ibby. "If he goes any further …" She trailed off uneasily.

"What's the matter?" said Francis. "What comes after Phase Four?"

"Nothing. That's the trouble. The Life Cycle ends at Phase Four."

"You mean … oh!"

There was a sombre silence while they

imagined what might happen if Alex went beyond Phase Four. Would he die? Would he vanish in a puff of smoke? Or would he just crumble away, leaving nothing but a pile of second-hand clothes?

"Is that what happened to Uncle Godfrey?" asked Francis.

Ibby looked at Francis, shocked. Now that he mentioned it, Ibby realized that she didn't really know what had happened to their Uncle Godfrey. Her mother had told her that he'd disappeared – but how, exactly? What if Francis was right? What if one of Uncle Godfrey's magic tricks had gone wrong? And what if the same thing happened to Alex!

They were both still sitting there wondering what to do when the doorbell rang. They jumped, and looked at one another in alarm. Was that Aunt Carole back again? Or was it news of something even worse? They both got up and ran to the door to find DI Davies and PC Preston standing on the doorstep. PC Preston was carrying what appeared to be a bundle of clothes with a top hat balanced on the top.

Ibby gasped and clapped her hand over her

mouth. It was just as they'd suspected! Alex had completely disappeared and left only his clothes behind.

"What happened?" cried Francis.

DI Davies shifted awkwardly. "Well, that's the thing," he said. "We're not sure. One minute he was there; the next he was gone."

At this, Ibby let out a cry, and Francis's eyes filled up with tears.

"Don't worry," said DI Davies reassuringly. "He won't get far without his clothes."

"What we want to know," said PC Preston, "is where the baby came from."

Ibby looked up. "Baby?" she said. "What baby?"

PC Preston lifted the top hat and there, swamped in clothes that were far too large for it, was a baby. He had round brown eyes and a dark wisp of hair on the crown of his head.

"When I put my foot on the brakes," said DI Davies, "we heard a thump, like something rolling off the back seat, followed by a wail."

"And when we looked in the back," said PC Preston, "there he was. On the floor. I don't suppose you recognize him?"

Ibby and Francis studied the baby closely.

As they peered at him, he smiled and thrust a chubby hand in their direction.

"It's him!" said Francis suddenly. "It's Alex!"

"Oh!" cried Ibby. "Of course!" And she went to take baby Alex from PC Preston's arms.

"Just a minute," said PC Preston. In her experience, relatives usually recognized their babies much more readily than this. "Are you sure you know this baby?"

"I'd know him anywhere," said Francis cheerfully. "That's my brother, Alex."

DI Davies and PC Preston exchanged uncertain glances.

"Well ... if you're sure," said PC Preston.

"We are," said Ibby.

And so, since neither PC Preston nor DI

Davies wanted to return to the station with a wailing baby, PC Preston put Alex into Ibby's outstretched arms, then they got back in their police car and drove away again.

"Now what?" said Ibby, when they were back inside.

"Now we make him do the trick again," said Francis simply. "Then he'll be back where he started!"

"How are we going to make him do that? He can't speak!"

Francis frowned. He hadn't thought of that. It would be at least two years before Alex was able to do the trick again.

"This is even worse than before," said Ibby wretchedly. "What's Aunt Carole going to say?"

"Perhaps she'll be pleased," said Francis. "She likes babies."

Francis quite liked the idea of having a baby brother – and since he was now the eldest it was only fair that he should have Alex's computer and metal detector. After all, Alex wouldn't be able to use them, would he? In fact, the easiest solution was simply to swap rooms. A baby would be glad of all his toys, thought Francis, even if a lot of them were broken.

Francis's plans were interrupted by a muffled trumpeting sound from the baby's lower half, followed by an awful smell.

"Ugh!" cried Ibby. She held Alex at arm's length and hurried back and forth as though searching for a place to set him down. Eventually, she bolted upstairs to the bathroom. Francis hesitated, then he hurried after her.

Changing a baby is a messy business – especially when it isn't wearing a nappy. From behind the closed bathroom door there came exclamations of disgust and groans of dismay – and above it all rose Alex's wails. But eventually the door opened and out they came with Alex wearing an enormous nappy fashioned from a towel. He was still crying.

"Let's put him to bed," said Ibby. "Maybe he'll sleep it off."

So they put Alex in his own bed, drew the curtains and turned out the light. But no sooner had they shut the door on his wails than there came another sound – the sound of the front door opening and Aunt Carole's voice calling cheerfully, "Hello! Is anyone home?"

"She's back!" said Ibby, turning pale.

They rushed to the top of the stairs to see

Aunt Carole unbuttoning her coat in the hall. "What's that noise?" she said. "Is everything all right?"

"Fine!" said Francis.

"Fine? It doesn't sound fine. It sounds like a baby crying."

"It's all right. It's only Alex."

"Alex?" said Aunt Carole, puzzled. And before they could prevent her she had climbed the stairs and marched along the corridor to Alex's room.

The crying appeared to have stopped.

"Alex?" said Aunt Carole. "Are you all right?" She knocked softly and opened the door, and a path of light fell across the bed and onto the pillow. And there was Alex, sound asleep, sucking his thumb – and practically a teenager again."

Alex finally emerged at dinner time. He'd had a shower and was pale and careful, like someone who is out of bed for the first time after a long illness. He sat at the table with his hair still damp and combed neatly to one side, and ate his tomato soup in silence. Afterwards he excused himself and went upstairs again.

"Alex doesn't seem himself tonight," remarked Aunt Carole thoughtfully. "I hope there's nothing the matter."

"Oh – just growing pains," said Ibby reassuringly.

Francis gave a snort of laughter, which made tomato soup come out of his nose and sent them both into fits of giggles.

"Oh, Francis!" said Aunt Carole, handing him a tissue. She could never understand the sort of things that Francis found so funny.

CHAPTER 14

Uncle Godfrey
"THE PROFESSIONAL MAGICIAN NEVER REVEALS HIS SECRETS."

"It's your last day tomorrow," said Aunt Carole.

"Yes," reflected Ibby. She and her aunt were playing snakes and ladders in front of the fire. Alex and Francis had already gone to bed.

"Has it gone quickly?"

"Yes," said Ibby. "Quicker than I thought it would." It was strange to think how much she had been dreading coming here. But everything had turned out all right in the end, hadn't it? Alex and Francis weren't that bad, she thought. You had to get used to them, that was all. And they had done nearly all the magic tricks now. The only ones left were the card tricks and the Vanishing Act – but the Vanishing Act wouldn't work without the padlock, and you couldn't get into much trouble with cards, could you?

"Your turn," said Aunt Carole.

Ibby threw the dice and moved her counter forwards – one, two, three. It would seem quiet at home, she thought, without her cousins.

Aunt Carole shook the dice, then cast it on the board. "Five!" she said, and moved her counter forwards. But unfortunately, the fifth move landed her on the head of a snake, which meant she had to go all the way back to the bottom.

Ibby yawned.

"I think we can safely say that you have won," Aunt Carole said. "Shall we call it a day?"

"OK," said Ibby.

So Aunt Carole raked the ashes and put the fireguard on, and Ibby went to put the board game back in the cupboard.

It was while she was closing the cupboard door that Ibby noticed the photograph on the dresser. It was very like her mother's graduation portrait – the one where she was sitting against a mottled blue background wearing a black cloak and a flat black hat called a mortarboard. But this photo was of Uncle Godfrey. He was also wearing a cloak, but instead of a mortarboard he was wearing a tall top hat, and instead of a rolled-up degree certificate, he was holding a slender black wand with white tips. He was beaming.

"That's your Uncle Godfrey," said Aunt Carole, smiling. "He'd just been granted entry to the Magic Circle."

Ibby knew all about the Magic Circle. Every magician wanted to belong to it. The Magic Circle made its members promise not to tell anyone how they did their magic tricks. Ibby had always assumed that this was because they didn't want people to know that they were only doing tricks – but now she suspected it was because they didn't want people to know that they were doing real magic.

"He'd wanted to be a magician since he was fourteen," said Aunt Carole. "He was always sending away for books and things, and practising in his room. Your grandmother disapproved. She wanted him to be a doctor."

There was a pause while they studied the photograph thoughtfully. Then Ibby said, "Aunt Carole, was Uncle Godfrey a *real* magician?"

"A professional, you mean? Oh, yes! He did children's parties, mainly. And he performed tricks just outside Piccadilly Station and collected money in his top hat."

"Yes," said Ibby. "But was he—"

"I've got some pictures here!" Aunt Carole selected a fat album from the top shelf, and opened it at random. "There's Godfrey," she said, pointing to a boy of about Alex's age. He was standing proudly in a kitchen wearing a top hat that was slightly too large for him, and his ears stuck out at right angles. "And that's him there," said Aunt Carole, pointing him out in a group of men in black top hats and satin cloaks, standing on the steps of a very grand building. "It was his first year at the Academy." She flipped forwards again, and there were photographs of picnics on the beach and

117

Christmas mornings round the tree, and Uncle Godfrey was in lots of them. And then, quite suddenly, he no longer appeared.

"Aunt Carole," said Ibby. "What happened to Uncle Godfrey?"

Aunt Carole hesitated. "He had an accident. A silly, silly accident." Something in her voice made Ibby glance up, and she saw that her aunt's eyes were full of tears.

"Take no notice of me," said Aunt Carole, smiling. "I miss him sometimes, that's all."

She busied herself putting the album back up on the shelf – but as she did so several pieces of paper slipped out and fluttered to the floor. Ibby went to pick them up. They were tickets from magic shows, and postcards with Uncle Godfrey's spiky handwriting on them – and there was a yellowing newspaper article too. Ibby just caught the headline: MAGICIAN DISAPPEARS, before Aunt Carole took the papers out of her hands and shoved them hastily back between the pages of the album.

"Look at the time!" Aunt Carole exclaimed. "You'd better get to bed."

Ibby hesitated.

"Go on," said Aunt Carole. "You can use the

bathroom first."

Reluctantly, Ibby went upstairs. What was it that Aunt Carole hadn't wanted her to see? Her aunt was hiding something from her, she was sure of it.

After she had gone to bed Ibby lay for a long time with her eyes wide open in the dark. She heard Aunt Carole's footsteps on the stairs, then she heard the bathroom door shut and water splashing in the sink. Then she heard Aunt Carole go round switching out the lights. Only when the line of light had disappeared from under her bedroom door did Ibby lift back her covers and slip noiselessly out of bed. As quietly as she could, she opened her door and crept downstairs.

The fire in the front room was dying in the grate; its orange coals gave just enough light to see by. Ibby pulled a chair across to the bookshelf and stood on it to reach the photo album. Then she went and knelt on the hearthrug and shook the album upside down. The tickets and postcards fluttered out onto the rug – and there was the newspaper article. Ibby read it in the light from the coals. Here is what it said:

MAGICIAN DISAPPEARS

Police are investigating the disappearance of a children's entertainer. Magician Godfrey Grubb disappeared at a birthday party last night at a residence in Gannock Park. Eyewitnesses report that the event occurred near the end of the show, when the magician climbed into a trunk as part of a "Vanishing Act". Birthday boy Alistair Sheldon was invited to play the part of the magician and make him disappear.

When the boy was unable to bring the magician back again, Alistair's parents called the police.

"It really ruined the party," said Mrs Sheldon. "The children were very upset."

Police are asking anyone who might have seen a tall man in the locality, wearing a black top hat and a satin cloak, to please come forward.

So Uncle Godfrey hadn't just disappeared
– he'd vanished! And the boy must not have
been able to bring him back again. Poor Uncle
Godfrey! But how silly he had been – imagine
letting someone shut you in a box!

Just then there came the creak of floorboards
overhead. Quickly, Ibby stuffed the article into
the pocket of her nightdress, returned the album
to the shelf and hurried back upstairs. She closed
her bedroom door softly, slipped back into bed
and lay very still. The house was quiet. Only the
thumping of her heart and the slight crinkle of
paper in the pocket of her nightie betrayed the
fact that she'd been out of bed at all.

CHAPTER 15

The Vanishing Act

"ALL MAGIC TRICKS ARE UNDERTAKEN AT THE MAGICIAN'S OWN RISK."

When Ibby next opened her eyes it was early morning, and the house was still. She jumped out of bed, put on her rabbit slippers and hurried down the corridor to Francis's room.

"Francis!" she hissed, shaking him by the shoulder. "Wake up!"

Francis opened his eyes. "Huh?"

"I found out what happened to Uncle Godfrey. He didn't just disappear – he vanished."

"What?"

"He vanished!"

"Vanished?" said Francis. "How?"

But instead of explaining, Ibby turned and rushed out of the room. Francis threw back his covers and followed. Ibby went straight down the corridor to Alex's room and walked in without knocking. Then she yanked the curtains open, letting in the light.

"Hey!" protested Alex, clutching at his duvet. "What do you think you're doing?"

"Look," said Ibby, handing him the newspaper article. "It's about Uncle Godfrey. He vanished."

Alex read the article thoughtfully.

"It's the Vanishing Act," said Ibby. "The one from the magic set. It has to be."

"Yes," reflected Alex. "Something must have gone wrong and the boy couldn't get him back again."

While the others were talking, Francis had been reading the article. He was a slower reader than Alex, and there were words that he hadn't seen before. "What's a trunk?" he asked.

"It's like a pirate's treasure chest," said Ibby. "Look – that's it, in the picture."

"Is that the one that Uncle Godfrey vanished in?"

"Yes."

Francis studied the picture thoughtfully. "It's just like the one in the attic."

The others stared at him. "There's a trunk like this in the attic?" cried Ibby.

Francis nodded.

Alex and Ibby looked at one another. Was it possible? Could it be the very same trunk that Uncle Godfrey had climbed into all those years ago? And could it be that he was somehow still inside it?

"Perhaps he's waiting to be brought back," said Ibby.

"What – five years later?" said Alex, doubtfully.

"Maybe."

"And even if he is still in there," said Alex. "We won't be able to get him back again."

"Why not? We've still got the key, haven't we?"

"Yes – but we haven't got the padlock."

"Yes, we do," said Francis.

"We do?"

Francis nodded. "It's on the trunk."

Ibby and Alex stared at Francis.

Then Alex jumped out of bed and threw on his dressing gown. Ibby got the Magic for Beginners set out from the bottom of the wardrobe and, very quietly, they all tiptoed out of the room and down the corridor. They came to a halt on the landing, directly underneath the hatch to the attic.

"You really think he's up there?" whispered Ibby.

But before the others could answer, a door opened at the other end of the corridor and out came Aunt Carole, yawning and securing the belt of her dressing gown. "You're up early," she remarked. "What are you all doing?"

For a moment nobody spoke. Then Francis startled everyone by hurrying forwards, waving his arms and shouting: "No! Go back! Go back!"

"What for?" cried Aunt Carole.

"We're making you breakfast in bed!"

"Oh!" said Aunt Carole, delighted. "Isn't that nice." And she allowed Francis to shepherd her back into her room. The others breathed a sigh of relief as he closed her door again.

"Good thinking, Francis," said Alex.

Francis stiffened proudly.

Breakfast was a team effort. Alex filled the kettle and Francis put bread in the toaster. Then Ibby arranged everything on a tray and within minutes they were all heading solemnly upstairs again. They found Aunt Carole sitting up with lots of pillows at her back. "I feel like the Queen!" she said. Alex set the tray on her lap, then they all hurried back to the landing.

The hatch to the attic was the sort that you pull open with a long pole with a hook on one end. Alex seized the pole, which was standing against the wall, and hooked the metal ring. When he pulled the hatch open, an aluminium ladder slid out, and when it was within reach the others drew it down until it reached the floor. Then they stood there, peering at the black square in the ceiling.

"Who wants to go first?" said Alex.

"I will!" said Francis bravely. But first he ran to get his caving helmet with the light attached to the front. Ibby fastened the chin strap for him, then he put one bare foot on the first rung and began climbing.

The worst part about going into any attic is the moment when your head first goes through the hatch. This is the moment in which you feel especially vulnerable. If there was anything up there waiting for you, this would be the moment it would pounce.

Glad he was wearing a helmet, Francis put his head up through the opening and looked about. Nothing pounced. The beam of his head torch flashed over the rafters and threw crazy shadows from stacks of cardboard boxes, old lampshades, and piles of books.

"All right?" called Alex from below.

Francis gave the thumbs-up, and a moment later the ladder started juddering as Ibby climbed up after him, carrying the magic set. She was followed by Alex. Presently all three of them were standing in the attic in their pyjamas, looking round like explorers in an undiscovered cave.

Attics are forgotten places. They are full of ancient cobwebs and hopeless flies buzzing at skylights that never open. Attics are also full of secrets, and Aunt Carole's attic had never felt more full of secrets than now.

"Follow me," said Francis. He led them to the far side of the attic where the eaves came down so low that they had to stoop to avoid banging their heads. "It's under here," he said, and he lifted up one corner of a dusty sheet and drew it back.

The sheet was covering a pile of things, all stacked untidily: a folding card table, an empty birdcage and a long dark box with a large hole in one end. "That's one of those boxes for sawing people in half," said Ibby with a shiver. Then Francis said, "Here it is!" and together they pulled out a large wooden trunk, covered in a layer of dust. On the front of the trunk

swung a large gold padlock. It was open.

It is not pleasant opening a trunk that hasn't
been opened for years and years – especially
when you don't know what will be inside.
Cautiously, Alex removed the padlock. Then he
lifted the lid and peered in. "Empty!" he said,
relieved.

Now that they were looking at it, it was hard
to believe that Uncle Godfrey could somehow
still be in there, waiting to reappear.

"What if he comes back dead?" said Francis
anxiously.

"What – like a ghost?" said Alex.

"Or a skeleton."

Alex and Ibby looked at one another

doubtfully. Neither of them wanted to bring back
a dead body. But for Uncle Godfrey's sake they
couldn't leave without trying.

"Come on," said Ibby. "Quick. Before Aunt
Carole gets up."

So Alex closed the lid, replaced the padlock
and pressed it shut with a click. Now it wouldn't
open without the key.

"Who's going to do the trick?" said Alex.

"I will," said Ibby.

Alex looked at Ibby in surprise. "Are you sure?"

"Of course I'm sure." Ibby opened the magic
set, lifted out the plastic tray and removed the
black top hat. She popped it up and put it on.
Next, she shook out the black satin cloak and
draped it round her shoulders. She caught sight
of herself then, in a mirror propped against a
chair, and she paused to lift her long fair hair
and let it fall over her black satin shoulders. She
hardly recognized herself. Her face looked small
and pale under the brim of the black top hat, and
she stood taller and straighter than usual.

"First tip your hat to the ladies," said Alex,
consulting the instruction booklet.

Ibby tipped her hat at her reflection.

"Not like that – like this," said Alex.

Ibby tried again.

The next step said: Show the key to the audience, so Ibby held up the little gold key and showed it to Alex and Francis. Then she signalled at Francis to pass her the wand.

Francis was careful to put the wand into her hand the right way round. It made her fingertips tingle, as though there was a faint electric current running through it. Ibby glanced at the booklet again and then, with the wand, she drew three neat figure-of-eights above the trunk and tapped the lid once, twice, three times. "REAPPEAR!" she cried. And then, with trembling fingers, she put the gold key in the lock, and turned it.

The padlock clicked open.

Ibby removed the padlock, then stood well back, as though expecting Uncle Godfrey to burst out at any moment like a jack-in-the-box. But nothing happened.

"I knew it wouldn't work," muttered Alex.

Ibby lifted the lid a fraction, and peered inside.

"What can you see?" asked Alex.

"Nothing," said Ibby, squinting.

"Let me have a look," said Francis. The light from his head torch shone into the dark interior of the trunk and fell upon the gleaming white of an eye. The eye swivelled.

Ibby screamed and dropped the lid, and they all scrambled backwards to a safe distance.

"He's in there!" whispered Ibby. "He was looking at me!"

"What's he waiting for?" said Alex. "Why doesn't he open the lid?"

"Perhaps he's waiting for the signal."

"What signal?"

"To tell him it's time to come out."

But since none of them wanted to go near the trunk again, Alex hunted about and found a broom and, standing at arm's length, he hooked it under the edge of the lid and flipped it open. The lid flew back with a crash, raising a cloud of dust that twinkled in the torchlight – and there, hugging his knees to his chest and keeping very still, was …

"Uncle Godfrey?" said Ibby.

It was Uncle Godfrey all right – who else could it have been? He sat up, blinking and

squinting in the light from Francis's torch. His hair stood straight up like a brush, and his ears stuck out.

"Did it work?" he asked.

The children stared at him, not knowing what to say.

"What's going on?" said Uncle Godfrey. "Where's Alistair?"

"Alistair couldn't get you back," said Alex.

"Couldn't get me back?" Uncle Godfrey climbed stiffly out of the trunk and looked around. He was wearing a crumpled black suit which stopped just short of his wrists and ankles. "What is this place?" he said. "Where am I?" Only a moment ago, it had seemed, he had been in Mr and Mrs Sheldon's sunny living room.

"We're in the attic," Ibby told him. "At Aunt Carole's house."

Uncle Godfrey looked at Ibby in the black top hat and satin cloak, and frowned. "And who are you?"

"I'm Ibby."

"Who?"

"Your niece. And these are your nephews, Alex and Francis."

Uncle Godfrey peered at them. "Alex?" he said. "Is that really you?"

Alex nodded.

"Good Lord!" said Uncle Godfrey. (The last time he had seen Alex, the boy had only been seven.) "How long have I been in there?"

"Five years," said Alex.

"Five years?" Uncle Godfrey laughed incredulously. "Surely not!"

"Show him the article, Ibby," said Alex.

So Ibby produced the newspaper article and Uncle Godfrey got a pair of glasses out of his shirt pocket and read it in the light from Francis's torch. When he'd finished he put his glasses away and shook his head. "Five years?" he repeated.

"We thought you were dead!" said Francis.

Uncle Godfrey's forehead wrinkled. "Oh dear," he said. He scratched his head and looked around. "Where's Carole?"

"She's in bed," said Alex. "She doesn't know you're back."

"Well, what are we waiting for?" cried Uncle Godfrey. "Let's go!"

So Francis packed up the magic set and they all made their way back across the attic, down the ladder and along the corridor to Aunt Carole's room. Alex knocked twice.

"Come in!" called Aunt Carole.

Alex opened the door.

When Aunt Carole saw her brother standing there, she gave a shriek and dropped her cup of tea. It rolled across the duvet, spilling everywhere, but Aunt Carole took no notice. "Godfrey!" she cried, and she leaped out of bed and threw her arms around him. A moment later she was holding him at arm's length to take a better look. "You're back!" she said. "But where …? How …?"

"It was the children," said Uncle Godfrey, beaming. "They completed the trick! They brought me back again."

Aunt Carole stared at them, astonished. Then her eyes fixed on the magic set. "You mean you found the magic set? You did the Vanishing Act?"

"You knew about it?" cried Alex.

"Of course!"

"You never told us!"

Aunt Carole looked uncomfortable. "No. Perhaps we should have. But we didn't want any more magicians in the family – not after what happened to your uncle."

"Does Mum know too?" asked Ibby.

Aunt Carole nodded.

"But if you knew about the magic set," said Alex, "why didn't you try to bring Uncle Godfrey back yourselves?"

"We did!" said Aunt Carole. "At first we didn't know what had happened – Godfrey hadn't told us how his tricks were done. But when the police returned his magic set and all his other props, we found the Magic for Beginners instruction booklet. Well – it was all there, wasn't it, in black and white? The Vanishing Act! So we tried it – lots of times – but nothing worked. Uncle Godfrey never reappeared. We did our best, but we're not magicians."

"Couldn't another magician have helped?" asked Ibby.

Aunt Carole shook her head. "They didn't want to get involved for legal reasons."

"What about the Magic Circle?"

"They were very sorry, they said, but all magic tricks were undertaken at the magician's own risk, and it was their policy not to divulge their methods to members of the public."

"The less people know about magic, the

better," said Uncle Godfrey. "It's the only way to prevent it falling into the wrong hands."

Francis had been listening thoughtfully. Now, for the first time, he spoke. "Maybe," he said, "you weren't holding the wand the right way round."

Aunt Carole blinked. "There's a right way round?"

"Of course!"

At this, Aunt Carole looked so dismayed that Uncle Godfrey laughed and put his arm around her shoulders. "Not to worry," he said. "You did your best."

Aunt Carole shook her head. To think that all this could have been avoided if only Godfrey hadn't climbed into that trunk! "Whatever made you let that boy do the Vanishing Act in the first place?" she said.

Uncle Godfrey looked sheepish. "It was his birthday."

"Well, never mind," said Aunt Carole. "You're back now. That's the main thing. Let's go down and have a cup of tea."

So they proceeded downstairs – a happy but dishevelled group, with Uncle Godfrey in his crumpled suit and the others in their pyjamas.

But they were only halfway down the stairs
when the doorbell rang and a familiar voice
called through the letterbox, "Yoo-hoo! Is
anybody home!"

Ibby ran down the last few stairs and along
the hall. "It's Mum and Dad!" she cried.
"They're back!"

CHAPTER 17
Advanced Magic
"CAUTION: SOME EXPERIENCE NECESSARY."

It was unfortunate that the first thing Ibby's mother saw when the door opened was Ibby smiling proudly in the black top hat and satin cloak. Just behind her was Uncle Godfrey, waving cheerfully.

Ibby's mother's smile faded. She went very white, and then she closed her eyes and sank gracefully to the ground.

"Good Lord!" said Uncle Godfrey. "She's fainted!" He and Ibby's father picked her up and carried her inside. They laid her on the couch and slapped her cheeks, and eventually her

141

eyes opened. She looked first at Uncle Godfrey, whom she had never thought to see again, and then at Ibby, who she barely recognized beneath the brim of the black top hat. Then her lids fluttered for the second time, and her head lolled to one side.

"Good Lord!" said Uncle Godfrey. "She's fainted again!"

"A cup of tea is what she needs," Aunt Carole said, and she ran to the kitchen to put the kettle on.

Moments later, Ibby's mother was revived by the sounds of the tea tray arriving and the tea being poured. She sat up, blinked, and said, "Godfrey? Is that really you?"

"Yes, Ruth," he said. "It is."

There were exclamations, hugs and tears then, of course. Ibby's father shook Uncle Godfrey's hand and clapped him on the shoulder, and Uncle Godfrey said, "Has it really been five years?" And Ibby's father said yes, and yet Uncle Godfrey didn't look as though he'd aged a day.

"But where have you been?" cried Ibby's mother.

"In the trunk!" said Uncle Godfrey cheerfully.

"How did you get back?"

"The children rescued me."

"The children?"

"Yes!"

And then everyone began talking at once. Ibby's mother listened with her eyes growing wider and wider, until they got to the part about Ibby waving the magic wand and opening the trunk and finding Uncle Godfrey still inside.

"Ibby brought you back?" she said, and she looked at Ibby standing there in the black top hat and satin cloak as though seeing her properly for the first time.

"Yes," said Uncle Godfrey, putting his arm round Ibby's shoulders. "We'll make a magician of you yet – won't we, Ibby?"

"You will not!" said Ibby's mother. Uncle Godfrey laughed.

"What I'd like to know," said Aunt Carole, "is how you found the magic set in the first place."

"That was Francis," said Alex.

They told their parents everything then – about Francis shrinking himself, and Alex levitating out of the window, about Francis disappearing and Alex growing up. "This explains a lot!" said Aunt Carole. And Francis got overexcited and leaped around the room flourishing the wand and re-enacting everything.

"Put that thing down!" said Aunt Carole, laughing. "You'll have someone's eye out!"

So Francis threw the wand onto the couch and helped himself to a chocolate-covered wafer.

"But what I don't understand," said Ibby's mother, accepting a cup of tea, "is why the trick didn't work when *we* tried it."

"Apparently," said Aunt Carole, "we were holding the wand the wrong way round. The end with the short white tip is the end you hold."

"But that's ridiculous!" cried Ibby's mother. "The long white end should be the handle."

Francis shook his head. "That's the end you tap things with."

"Every time we did the trick," explained Aunt Carole, "we must have been making ourselves reappear – not Godfrey."

"No wonder it gave me a headache," muttered Ibby's mother.

Aunt Carole laughed. "Tea, Gerald?"

"Yes, please," said Ibby's father, and he took the cup and sat down on the couch. But as he sat down there was a sharp crack. It was the

unmistakable sound of something snapping
– something long and stick-like, and probably
made of wood.

"What was that?" he said, jumping up again.

Everyone stopped talking and looked round.
The wand was lying on the couch where Francis
had thrown it – and it was shaped like an L. For
a moment nobody moved. Then Francis gave a
cry of anguish. He seized the wand and tried to
straighten it – but it was no use. As soon as the
wand was flourished – even gently – it collapsed
and dangled from a splinter.

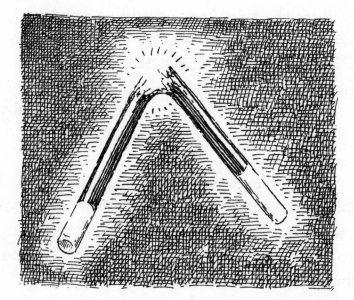

"I'm very sorry," said Ibby's father. "I didn't see it there."

"Never mind," said Ibby's mother. "It's probably just as well."

Francis's chin began to tremble. He drew a deep, unsteady breath, and began sobbing quietly.

"Oh, dear," said Ibby's father. "Perhaps it can be fixed."

Uncle Godfrey looked doubtful, but Ibby's father took Francis into the kitchen and they tried to mend the wand with electrical tape. It wasn't any use. Everyone knew that it would never work again. And without the wand the magic set was worthless. They had already lost the Disappearing Coin and the hand mirror, and none of the other tricks would work without the wand.

"Never mind," said Uncle Godfrey. "We can still do card tricks."

But card tricks weren't much consolation.

"Have another biscuit," said Aunt Carole. But Francis didn't want one. He went and sat at the end of the couch, nursing the broken wand and snuffling miserably. Alex sat down opposite, staring gloomily into his orange juice.

Ibby hated seeing her cousins like this – it wasn't like them at all. And despite the trouble it had given them, she couldn't help feeling disappointed that the wand had broken. Amazing Miniaturization would have been perfect for making dolls' house furniture. Just think of it – proper chests of drawers with tiny handles and all the things inside much tinier than you could ever buy them in a shop.

Over a second cup of tea, it was decided that Ibby and her parents would stay with Aunt Carole for a few days, and bring Uncle Godfrey up to date on all their news. So Aunt Carole took the empty cups back to the kitchen, and Ibby's parents and Uncle Godfrey went outside to bring the cases in.

"Well," said Alex, once they were alone. "That's the end of that then." He picked up the magic set. "I suppose we'd better put it back."

But Francis didn't want to let go of the wand.

"Come on, Francis," said Ibby gently. "It's broken. It doesn't work any more."

Francis sniffed and wiped his nose with his sleeve, then reluctantly he put the wand back in the plastic tray. It was a tight fit now, with the electrical tape around its middle.

"And the hat," said Alex.

Ibby had forgotten that she was still wearing the hat and cloak. She removed the black top hat and flattened it. Then she took off the satin cloak and folded it carefully. Alex lifted out the plastic tray so that she could put them underneath – and that was when they saw the piece of paper lying in the bottom of the box. It was strange they hadn't noticed it before.

"What's that?" said Ibby. She picked it up and turned it over. It was one of those glossy advertising flyers, the sort that slide out from between the pages of magazines, inviting you to subscribe for a year. As she read it, a smile spread slowly across her face.

"What does it say?" asked Francis.

Ibby showed them.

Magic for the More Advanced it said across the top, and there was a picture of a wizard with a long white beard and a pointy black hat with silver stars. He was flourishing a wand with glitter spilling from the end. Underneath was printed the following . . .

Amaze your friends and charm your girlfriend with Magic for the More Advanced! This set contains all the equipment you need to perform seven incredible magic tricks, including the world-renowned Indian Rope Trick and the ever popular Magic Carpet. Only £29.99, incl. p&p.

And that was all, except for a mailing address, and (in very small print) the words:

"CAUTION: SOME EXPERIENCE NECESSARY."